Princess

FROG-SNOGGER

by
Tommy Donbavand

Titles in Once Upon *Another* Time…

Badger Publishing Limited
Oldmedow Road,
Hardwick Industrial Estate,
King's Lynn PE30 4JJ

Telephone: **01438 791037**
www.badgerlearning.co.uk

2 4 6 8 10 9 7 5 3 1

Princess Frog-Snogger
ISBN 978-1-78464-520-5

Illustration: Mark Penman
Designer: Fiona Grant

Contents

Characters

Princess Ranida

Prince Gallant

Vocabulary

announced	kingdom
curse	peasants
decorated	population
exclaimed	sapphires
handsome	waded

Once Upon A Time...

Another

Chapter One
FROG-SNOGGER

Princess Ranida was wearing the most beautiful dress ever seen in the Kingdom of Bizarnia.

Layers of pretty lace matched her beautiful green eyes and her shoes were covered in sapphires and rubies.

This amazing outfit was worth more than most people earned in a year...

...and now it was covered in slime.

"Come here, you little beauty!" said the princess as she waded deeper into the village pond.

She eyed the large, green frog sitting on a lily pad just a few metres ahead of her. "Get ready for a great big kiss!"

The local peasants watched as Princess Ranida snatched up the frog, then planted her lips on its wet cheek and began to kiss it.

"*MMMMMWWWWAAAAHH!*"

The kiss over, Princess Ranida dropped the frog back on its lily pad and watched. It blinked twice, then fell into the water with a SPLASH.

"Nope! Just another frog!" she cried, climbing back out of the water. "I'll never find my handsome prince at this rate!"

"This one might be a prince, your highness..." said a scruffy boy among the crowd. In his hands, he held a tiny frog with yellow-green skin.

"What? That tiny thing?" scoffed the princess.

"Perhaps," said the boy.

"Oh, all right then!" said Ranida, bending to peck the tiny creature on its head.

Suddenly, there was a blinding flash of light and standing before the princess was a tall man with dark, perfect hair and a handsome face.

"I am Prince Gallant!" cheered the man. "You have freed me from the witch's curse!"

"*PHWOOOAAARRR!*"
cheered Princess Ranida.

Chapter Two
WEDDING

The marriage of Prince Gallant and Princess Ranida was planned for two weeks later.

All across Bizarnia, excitement grew at the thought of a royal wedding.

Houses were decorated with the royal colours, street parties were planned in villages and towns right across the land, and the local picture-on-a-china-mug factory announced record profits.

Finally, the big day arrived. Prince Gallant started by giving a speech to the crowds outside the palace.

"Citizens of Bizarnia," he announced. "As you know, I was cursed to live as a small, ugly frog for many years by the wickedest of all witches – Auntie Wartcream!"

The audience booed at the name of the kingdom's most-wanted witch.

"But now, I am back!" continued Prince Gallant. "And today, I marry my beautiful bride – Princess Ranida!"

The crowd cheered with joy as Ranida stepped out onto the balcony. She looked beautiful in a wedding dress made of pure silk.

The minister cleared his throat. "Prince Gallant, do you take Princess Ranida to be your wife?"

"I do!" said Prince Gallant, wiping away a tear.

"And Princess Ranida," said the minister. "Do you take Prince Gallant to be your husband?"

Princess Ranida paused for a second. Then...
"No," she said. "I don't."

The crowd gasped. The minister trembled. Prince Gallant nearly fainted.

"You see," said Princess Ranida, "after months of searching ponds and rivers for my handsome prince, I've discovered that I actually prefer kissing frogs!"

Then she turned and ran.

Chapter Three
WARTCREAM

Prince Gallant had been searching for his missing bride for almost a month when he met an old woman.

"The princess has been locked in the tall tower by Auntie Wartcream!" cackled the old woman.

"That hideous witch?" cried Gallant. "But, why?"

"Ranida went looking for the frog of her dreams," replied the old woman, "and she asked Wartcream to turn her into a croaker herself, piece by piece. She is her prisoner!"

Thanking the woman, Prince Gallant rode straight to the tall tower and threw Auntie Wartcream into a pond where she melted away into nothing.

"Ow!" said the witch, as she died.

"Ranida!" shouted the prince. "I have come to rescue you!"

"Oh, Gallant!" called Princess Ranida from the highest window. "I am sorry I ran away. I love you!"

"And I love you!" exclaimed Gallant. "Now, let down your hair and I shall climb up to you."

"I can't," sobbed Princess Ranida. "I had my hair cut short just yesterday!"

"Oh," said Prince Gallant.

"But," said Ranida. "The witch's spells have started to take effect – and I now have a very long tongue, just like a frog."

She leaned out of the window, said "**BLEURGH!**" and lowered a tongue that was at least 20 metres long.

Gripping this slimy, meaty rope, Prince Gallant began to climb.

"*AAAAARRRRGGGGHHHHH!*"

screamed the princess.

Eventually, the pair were together again. Prince Gallant swept Ranida into his arms.

"We shall be married this very day!" he said.

"**Watha thatha thith thoth!**" said Princess Ranida, stuffing her tongue back into her mouth.

And they both lived happily ever after, but didn't kiss much, because that would have been weird.

Story Facts

I've always been fascinated by fairy stories and the strange things that happen in them. Such as how Prince Charming manages to track down Cinderella using just her glass slipper. Is she really the only girl in the entire Kingdom to wear that size of shoe?

And how does Mummy Bear make one pot of porridge, then dish out three bowls of the stuff that are all at different temperatures?

Daddy Bear's porridge is too hot, so he makes the whole family go for a walk in the forest while it cools. Not exactly fair! By then, it's too late for Mummy Bear – her porridge is already too cold to eat, and Baby Bear's is just right, but it's all gone!

So, when I started to think about the story of *The Frog Prince*, I wondered what might happen if the princess decided that she preferred kissing frogs instead of humans. The result is this book!

Questions

Where is this story set? *(page 6)*

What did a scruffy young boy bring to the princess? *(page 10)*

Who nearly fainted on their wedding day? *(page 18)*

Where was Princess Ranida locked away? *(page 20)*

How long was Princess Ranida's new tongue? *(page 24)*

Meet the Author

Tommy Donbavand spent his school days writing stories in which more popular kids than him were attacked and devoured by slavering monsters. Years later, he's still doing the same thing – only now people pay him for it. The fools!

Meet the Illustrator

Mark Penman thinks he maybe played one too many fantasy games on his computer. Now it seems he can only silence the horrifying voices in his head by drawing scary stories starring terrified teens.